Rex sat on his rocking chair on his ricket
and cradling his shotgun. He was waitin
But some part of him, long buried benea
walks, self-isolation and lethargy, had re   ... ... was restless.
Twitchy.

There was no nobler impulse than survival. Rex had always known that. Hell, he'd lived his life in thrall to the sentiment; revered it like a religious commandment. Some might have labelled it unjust, even callous, to live life according to such binary precepts, but Rex was pretty sure that those who didn't agree with him on this were already dead, so who cared a god-damn what they thought.

Still, there were worse things out there in the world than death...

Rex hadn't seen the creatures for years, but he knew the cost of complacency - especially up here in the vast, unguarded emptiness of the mountains. Death wasn't the main enemy, it was erasure: the loss of a narrative he'd vowed he would keenly guard until there were historians once more in the world to record it. His way was the only way it could have been, and he never wanted mankind to forget that.

The virus, when it had struck all those years ago, hadn't just changed the rhythms of the world; it had changed great herds of its people, right down to their DNA. Mankind – the unlucky and the weak, at least - had been seized and moulded by a violent mutation, almost a micro-evolution: brought about by the virus, yes, but given shape and texture by the lack of food, medicine and toilet paper.

The thought of it forced another sliver of whiskey down Rex's throat.

In the years following the outbreak he and his people worked to stamp the creatures out wherever they amassed. Rex had called their gathering spots 'nests', and it had felt right, because they were savage, fast-breeding, inhuman vermin that would kill you as soon as look at you. Rex had never afforded them the chance to prove him wrong. His own people had always come first.

He'd had a few critics in the beginning, people who'd accused him of lacking both conscience and compassion. Almost without exception those people had found themselves expelled. Rex's kingdom was no place for those who wanted to reap the benefits of the life Rex had given them without ever getting their own hands dirty, preaching the evils of his methods to all who would listen. Fascists. Hypocrites. Cowards. He removed them like the cancerous polyps they were before they could infect the body of the camp. Why hadn't they understood?

It was simple: if you spent more time caring for your enemies than standing up for your own people, sooner or later you'd end up with a slit throat, and as a consequence heresy was a crime that Rex took very seriously.

It wasn't so easy to expel your own flesh and blood when they took the same position. That called for a different approach, one he'd had to take with Karl, his youngest son, and the brightest and biggest-hearted of his trio of boys.

One day, when Karl was around six or seven, he'd learned that Rex and his men were heading out to deal with a nest. Karl had heard stories from the other kids about the things that happened on his father's expeditions, and always seemed to struggle to reconcile the father he knew – the man who held him aloft on his shoulders, and told him stories and funny jokes – with the version of him everyone else seemed to know. And fear.

'You can't kill them, pop,' Karl had said, his little brow furrowed. 'They can't help the way they are.'

'Neither can rats,' Rex had told him. 'You wanna let them run free in your home? Nibble at your god damned toes?'

'But they're people, aren't they? Aren't they just like us?'

Rex had tousled his hair. Given him a sad smile. 'You let your heart bleed too much, son, you're gonna run out of blood.'

'But what if it was me who was out there?' Karl had asked.

The boy was sad, and a little scared, possibly the thought occurring to him for the first time that the violence of which he'd heard his father was capable might one day be visited upon him; an understandable fear, perhaps, but wholly unfounded. Rex had always been liberal of fist, and swift of gun, but he'd never once laid a hand on his boys, except to chide them if they ever strayed toward danger.

Karl searched for the same answer using a different question. 'Would you shoot me if I was one of them things, pop?'

'Boy,' he'd said, 'you aint, and never are gonna be, one of those things.'

'But why you gotta do it? Can't you just leave them be?'

Rex had brought down one of his big hands and rested it upon his son's shoulder: 'I do and we're all dead. We don't find them, they're gonna find us. What I do, I do it for you, boy.'

Karl's face had registered the impact of that answer. Rex could almost see the burden of the creatures' fate being passed to his son's bony shoulders, though the boy lacked the words and the wherewithal to comprehend the weighty transmission.

He'd watched the boy after that, made sure to tell him tales of the creatures' attacks, draw him into the confidence of the group's older members. Eventually, Rex had started taking him out on hunts, worked up to letting him pull the trigger. Bullets could tear people apart, but they could also bond them.

Only once had he let his son's kindness and pure heart affect his decision-making, and he'd never breathed a word about it to another living soul. A leader had to lead - decisively, consistently and without falter - else he wasn't fit to lead. People could smell weakness. And no one liked a bad smell.

Rex sighed. It all seemed so far behind him now. Another life almost.

He'd been right about it all, of course. Everything that had happened, everything he'd done; not just his stance on the creatures, but the whole god damned lot of it. He was sure. History would prove it; as would the mere fact of his continuance.

Yes... he'd been right.

Hadn't he?

Lately, the doubt had set into his bones like gout. He always tried to shake it off, but it didn't always work. With age comes wisdom, as the old saying goes, but to Rex age had brought only fracture; confusion.

Uncertainty.

Something else was troubling him: they were late. They'd been late before, but only by a matter of days. Never this late. Never five weeks. Still... the last few months had been unseasonably rainy. He was up in the mountains sheltered by forests, so the effects on him had been negligible, but the deluge would have caused problems for the network (his network, as he still liked to think of it) of towns and villages in the valley miles below him.

He surveyed his territory, always vast and breath-taking in the daylight, but stifling and claustrophobic after dusk. The sky was starting to darken above the mountains. A bitter breeze tormented the trees. He could have been – and perhaps should have been – sitting by the fire in his cabin, reading one his books about a world that no longer was. Call it instinct; call it foreboding, but something in his gut told him to keep watch. He rewarded his gut with more whiskey, grateful for the scratch of warmth in his old gullet as it went down. The glass drained, he placed it gently on the circular table at his side.

The wars were long since over. They'd been violent, seismic. Chaos and panic brought to the boil, exploding in riots and hangings and coups, until the fire had caught hold and burned proper, scorching away families, childhoods, countries and whole ways of life.

The virus had taken everyone by surprise. Certainly no-one could have predicted that a single pack of toilet paper would light the touch-paper on a Darwinian battle for survival.

That's how it had started: the stock-piling. Immediately before the country-wide lockdown - which everyone had known was on the cards - people had started clamouring to the shops like licensed looters. The more toilet paper flew from the shelves, the more people panicked. The more people panicked, the more toilet paper they bought. And the more they panicked, the more they fought amongst themselves. Factories pumped up production; more and more trees were pulped to satisfy demand. Quotas were enforced, then ignored - and very rarely politely.

It was absurd in the beginning. Almost comedic. But the laughs didn't last long. Food came next, then medicines: a capitalist smash-grab sending an unbridgeable rift right down the middle of society. The virus spread so quickly, and with such devastating effects that the government, the military, the economy, couldn't keep pace and were eventually overwhelmed until, finally, they were subsumed by chaos.

Before long the hoarders were forming coalitions, consolidating their supplies and fending off the have-nots with increasing brutality. Toilet-paper factories were seized, as were slaughterhouses, distribution centres, farms, shops, chemists: all of them run by - and for - the victors.

If you were on one side of the rift: you died (if you were lucky). If you were on the other: you lived.

Rex had lived.

It was that simple.

When it came to a crisis, there was no such thing as society. Nor nations, nor treaties. Rex had learned that pretty quickly. And he'd exploited it. He'd been in charge, controlling a territory spanning hundreds of miles square or more. He'd made hard decisions: people had died; people had been killed; people had been left outside the circle of his protection to suffer the full force of the virus.

He wasn't proud of some of the things he'd done, sure, but he was a pragmatist. What he'd done, he'd done for himself and his family. Not just his flesh and blood, but his clan; his ties to them just as deep. He'd controlled a sprawling legion of men, women, and even children; commanded them to harvest what they needed by force. Very quickly his ranks had swollen with ex-police, ex-military, doctors, street thugs and hardened citizens of all stripes, and from all walks of life. As long as someone was strong, healthy and useful, they'd been welcome to join.

Rex had been a general, a prophet, a King, a father and a God all rolled into one. Now he wasn't sure exactly what he was. A figurehead?

A relic?

...Forgotten?

An owl hooted in the tree-tops. Rex jumped, almost knocking his glass to the ground. It bothered him that ears inured to gunfire and shells were now jumping at phantoms. Maybe it was his age. He'd never been a superstitious man, but something in his bones, something in his blood, had been screaming at him these past few weeks. Rustles here. Rustles there. Animal calls disturbing the tranquillity of an otherwise unremarkable blank and blue-skied day. It was like an angry God, hell-bent on judgement, had placed augurs everywhere for his torment.

Something took flight high up in the forest canopy, a percussive hiss of whipping wings and snapping twigs that caused Rex's heart to dance in his chest like a fish flopping in a bucket. He clutched at his shotgun, held the barrel in a vice-like grip. For a moment all he could hear were the laboured rasps of his own breathing.

Then the bells tinkled.

Maybe it had been the breeze, picking up and disturbing his network of strings - the air itself contriving him an augur to satisfy his new-found taste for paranoia - but something told him that the true answer would be less comforting.

His early warning system hadn't been triggered since he'd installed it a few years ago. The people of his tribe, who came to deliver food and supplies to him every month or so - his three sons amongst them - were always careful not to snag it. Rex hoped that they would come again soon. He was down to his last few packs of toilet paper, had little in the way of medicines, and the only food on the shelves in his pantry were tins of pasta and corned beef. He was too old to risk a long hike down the mountain trail. If anything went wrong, he'd be finished. Slowly, day by day, he was beginning to know fear and hunger: the dual foundations upon which his long-ago empire had been built.

At least he had plenty of whiskey.

Rex stood up, an effort at his age, but easier with all the adrenalin coursing through his body. He peered into the advancing gloom, trying to discern movement in the murk.

Nothing.

Even the breeze seemed to be standing still. Maybe an animal? ... The bells tinkled again, more insistently this time. No, not an animal. And not necessarily human either. Rex cocked his shotgun and strode to the edge of his stoop. He raised the barrel and pointed it into the darkness.

'I'd better see you out in the open by the count of three, dammit, or I'ma start blasting.'

His voice was swallowed up by the gloom.

If anything was out there, it was biding its time.

'I mean it,' he growled, his gruff and steady tone belying the unease squirreling in his gut. 'You think I survived out here all these years on my own thanks to my gift for diplomacy? One.'

He waited. 'Two.'

'Don't shoot,' came the voice.

A woman. Young. Although, given his age, 'young' was something of a catch-all term. Sixty-year-olds were young to him.

He swivelled the shotgun in the direction of her voice, keeping his arms firm and taut. No sense letting his guard down. Youth could be impetuous; dangerous. He'd been young once, too.

'I'm coming out now,' she said. 'Please don't shoot.'

She emerged from a nearby clump of trees, and moved slowly into the dome of light cast by the lamps hanging from Rex's cabin. Her arms were held high above her head. Rex followed her with the barrel of the gun. She certainly didn't fit the profile of a hiker or a wilderness wanderer. Her clothes were incongruously well-kept for the terrain and the hour – tan blazer, cream shirt, immaculately-pressed trousers. She looked more like a minor celebrity of old than a woman out on a mountain-top doing... whatever it was she'd been out there doing.

He supposed she was in her mid-twenties – though it was hard for a dinosaur like him to be sure. She had a heart-shaped face, framed by a waterfall of dirty-blonde hair, and a nervous gait, which wasn't really surprising given that a stern-faced old timer like him was currently training a gun on her.

And those eyes... man. They were something else... Dark. Almost empty.

'Do you think you could... you know, stop pointing that at me now?'

Rex snapped himself out of the canyon his thoughts had led him to. 'Are you alone?'

'I... what? Yes, of course I'm alone.'

'What you doin' out here?'

'I just need to rest and... and get my bearings. I'm lost.'

A silence stretched between them.

Rex stood deathly still, looking for all the world like a waxwork of a sheriff in a wild-west museum. The owl hooted again from the darkness just beyond them both. Rex didn't jump this time.

'Drop your pants,' he said.

'What?'

'You know what I said, and you know why I said it.'

'I will not,' she said.

Rex laughed. It was bitter, joyless. 'Lady, you don't drop your pants and your underwear in the next three seconds you're gonna have a lot more problems in your life than lousy navigation.'

She stood stoic and silent, either frozen with fright or busy calculating the possibilities. Rex wasn't sure what options the woman thought she had. There were only two.

To his relief, she brought her arms down to her hips, and started fumbling with the buttons on her trousers.

'Slowly,' he told her.

He watched as she slid her trousers and underwear down her legs, her body bending forward, her hair hanging down in a cascading veil. After a few seconds of patient fiddling she stood upright again.

Though she was naked from the waist down, it was her eyes, and not her exposed flesh, that most fascinated Rex. Despite her obvious discomfort and alarm, those eyes were shining as cold and brilliant as the mountain itself. Their intensity unnerved him. It was like looking into his own eyes, albeit as they'd been forty or so years ago. These days his eyes were misted with age and regret, the whites faded to a mottled grey, witness to their own gradual dissolution played out in cloudy slow-motion.

He looked down at the woman's crotch.

It'd been a long time since Rex had seen the female form, but he didn't permit himself a lapse into carnality. Too much was at stake. Besides, he wasn't sure he'd know what to do with it any more, or be able to muster much enthusiasm even if he did.

'Turn around,' said Rex. 'Slowly.'

The woman laughed; an exasperated bark.

'Lady, you sure don't know how to act around a man holding a loaded shotgun.'

Please just do what I say, he thought. *I ain't shot nothing but deer and rabbits for years, and I sure as shit ain't gonna break that streak shooting down a young girl.*

But he knew that he would. If he had to. For all he'd spent the last chunk of his dotage doing nothing more strenuous than sitting, thinking and drinking, he hadn't abandoned his nature. Or, rather, it hadn't abandoned him. The man he was, and always would be, was baked into his bones.

After what seemed like an eternity she turned around, allowing him to appraise the plump curves of her behind: two cheeks, perfectly proportioned, meeting in the middle like a couple of lop-sided parabolas.

He nodded to himself.

'Now bend over,' he shouted.

She obliged, seeming to take an almost theatrical bow as she did so.

Everything checked out.

Rex lowered the gun.

He could feel the whiskey burning back up his throat; he guessed that was the taste of relief.

'I guess you'd better come inside,' he said, starting towards the door of his cabin. 'But put your pants on. This ain't a nudist camp.'

~~

It was warm in the cabin. Bright. Cosy, even. Earthy and smoky from the fire. The world outside may have been loosely described as post-apocalyptic, but up here in the unspoiled wilderness, with electricity - generated by an adjacent wind turbine and solar panels on his roof- and a few mod cons, it was easy to forget that things had ever been any different.

Until strange women stumbled on your doorstep out of the blue...

Rex had put some music on as soon as they'd walked inside, careful first to safely lock the door behind him. He'd chosen a piece of orchestral music, something suitably light and innocuous. The music was more to quell his unease than to make the girl feel comfortable, but it seemingly failed at both. He saw her look around at his shelves, each of them filled with relics, photos and mementoes, a bemused but interested look on her face. He could guess why. Here he was, all alone, living a Spartan life in a cabin in the mountains, yet surrounded by the clutter and little trophies of a live lived... if not exactly 'well', then certainly 'long'. Nothing about his bearing or manner suggested sentimentality. His shelves carried all of that weight.

Her name was Corinne, she told him. She sat, rather stiffly and awkwardly, on one of his armchairs, her posture hinting at a chill she couldn't possibly be feeling in the almost tropical heat. Rex had propped his shotgun against the door, but couldn't yet bring himself to sit and relax. He poured himself another whiskey from the large standing cabinet on the back wall.

'I'm sorry about the... you know, making you do that. I took no pleasure in it.'

Any other girl would've made a wise-crack. Corinne just looked at him impassively.

'You wanna tell me what you're doing out here?' he asked.

'I guess... finding myself?'

Rex drained his glass in one. 'And yet you got lost.'

He smiled, but it wasn't reciprocated.

'Strange place and strange time for a stroll in the mountains,' he said, eyeing her. He went back to the cabinet to pour another glass.

She shook her head, gave a shy little smile, and then brought her legs up onto the seat and in towards her stomach. She looked small. Vulnerable. 'It's stupid. You know, I've been hearing all about the world, how it used to be, you know, from my dad, and all the other people in our camp, but... but they would never let me go out in it... to see for myself.'

Rex nodded. 'Because it's dangerous.'

He shuffled over to his armchair and sat down. His bones would normally be groaning with the effort, but the whiskey was keeping them quiet.

 'I know it was a foolish thing, but, you know... I was just so sick of stories. That's all they live on. It started to feel like they were all I had, too. And they weren't even my stories. You know? I... I just wanted to make some stories of my own.'

'The people in your camp. They know you're here?'

She shook her head.

'How'd you get here?'

'I took my dad's car. Spoke nicely to the man who guards the gate. My dad... he's... high up in the camp, it didn't take much to convince the guard. Everyone's a bit scared of him. My dad, that is.'

'But not you,' he said, with a wry smile. He took a sip of whiskey.

Corinne shrugged.

'So where's the car?'

'Hmmm?' said Corinne, looking momentarily perplexed.

'The car? You didn't drive it up the god damned mountain. Did it break down in the valley, run out of gas?'

'Oh, it... there was steam, you know, coming out of the engine. It's... you know, down on the road, down there.'

Rex straightened his back. 'That road's about a few hour's hike from here. Up steep slopes, through forests, over streams. Lady, you don't even look like you've broken a sweat, or so much as brushed against a tree.'

Corinne looked down at her feet, started rubbing at her wrist. She started to weep. 'I was so frightened. I've heard so many stories about... you know, those...those things out there. I guess... I dunno, I guess I was lucky finding you out here.'

Rex stared at Corinne, said nothing. Silence was often the best interrogator.

'You thought I was one of them, didn't you?' she asked, sniffling and wiping away a tear. 'When you first saw me?'

He nodded. 'You might not be one of them, but there's more to you than meets the eye, that's for god damned sure. But, at the very least, I think you're human. Very stupid. But human.'

Corinne rubbed at her nose. 'You ever seen one?'

Rex nodded, took a larger swig from his glass.

'What are they like?'

He considered the question a moment. How could he describe them? They were savage, without doubt. Cunning, almost certainly. Very few of them had a vocabulary much more advanced than that of a young child. Most of them just growled or wailed. They looked almost like people, but not quite. Stronger than your average person. He'd seen one break a man's arm with one swipe.

Their skin was pale, patchy, a weird hue of blue, darker in some of their kind than in others; some of them were even pinkish in tone; others still were dead ringers for real people, the only tell-tale difference in evidence below the waist. Sometimes they had deeply pronounced brows, lending them the look of Neanderthals. And, of course, they lacked the need or the ability to consume food or defecate, which was a fancy way of saying that they didn't eat or shit.

Long ago, a preacher in Rex's camp had dared to call Rex's treatment of the creatures 'an abrogation of the soul'.

'Father,' Rex had told him sternly, 'Those god damned things don't even have assholes, never mind souls.'

And they didn't. It was eerie. Literally inhuman.

Instead of eating like humans did, the creatures appeared to metabolise oxygen for sustenance. It was as chilling and ungodly as it was fascinating. Without the base building-blocks of things like eating and excreting - the little rituals and commonalities that tied mankind together - you were a robot; an alien; a creature. A monster. All they seemed to enjoy was killing.

'They look like us,' he said, 'More or less, give or take, but they're animals. No better or worse than wolves.'

Or rats...

Corinne slowly unfurled her legs, brought her feet down on the carpet.

'Have you, you know, ever killed one?'

Rex could feel her eyes burning into him. 'Yes,' he said, firmly.

'Why?'

'Why?' Rex spat. 'Would you kill a wolf if it was going for your damned throat?'

Corinne's mouth tightened. 'If we'd shot all the wolves,' she said, taking her time with the sentence, 'we'd never have had dogs.'

'Well if you want to find one of those things and break it in as a god damned pet, you be my guest, little lady, the door's just there.'

He could tell from her body posture, and also her youth – her stupid, idealised youth - that she was gearing up for a diatribe; a criticism, perhaps even a rejection, of him, and the way that he, and others like him, had handled the onset of the virus all those years ago. He was in no mood for idealism, nor to listen to the half-baked opinions of someone who'd spent her life cloistered from the new world, and wholly ignorant of the old. She could save her rebellious attitude for her daddy when she went back to him, tail between her legs.

'I'm... I'm sorry,' she said, fumbling with her fingers, her pugnacious spirit sputtering to nothing. 'I didn't mean to...'

'You look cold,' he said, pushing himself up from his seat. He made towards the kitchen, turning off the music and slamming his empty glass down on the side cabinet on the way. 'I'm gonna fix you some tea.'

'No,' she said.

He didn't turn to look back at her; just stood staring into the dark kitchen ahead of him.

'I just... you know, I wouldn't want you to go to any trouble,' she said.

'It's no trouble.'

Rex flicked on the light, stood for a couple of seconds mulling things over. Then walked back to get his shotgun.

He stood in the kitchen leaning his palms on the counter-top, the shotgun resting against the unit at his legs. It was cold in here, away from the warmth of the fire. He stared out the window at his own sorry reflection as it mingled with the murk of the mountain night. He looked old. Tired. A sunken sack of flesh; face scarred by wrinkles and covered in patches of stubble that grew over his face like grey moss. As the kettle boiled, he could hear Corinne getting up from the armchair and walking over to the large cabinet; heard her lifting some of the framed photographs and nick-knacks.

Something didn't add up about her. There she was, dressed in fine, near-immaculate clothes; nervy but bolshie, and with those god-damned eyes... still, it was an apocalypse out there, despite the long absence of war. Everyone was a bit kooky. She was probably just a coddled little girl trying to prove herself to daddy, no different from a thousand girls before her back when the world still held its shape. And who knows? She might yet prove useful. A new group to trade with, maybe. More supply routes, greater power for his sons to absorb or consolidate.

There were other groups out there, sure, most of them quite far-off, all with well-defined territories. Relations had been cordial.

That was mostly a testament to his sons running the largest camp for perhaps a thousand miles around or more, with enough man- and firepower at their disposal to repel even the most ambitious of incursions.

The kettle clicked off.

And just as it did so a dark shadow flitted across his vision. Something in the yard outside. He lurched for the light switch, flicked it off and hurried back to the window. Everything was still. Quiet. He stood there for a few seconds more, peering this way and that, before putting the light back on and picking up his shotgun.

In the living room, Corinne was standing at the window holding back a sliver of curtain, her face pressed to the glass.

'Get back from the window,' he barked.

She let the curtain go and backed away, a girlish look of panic upsetting her features. 'I... I heard a noise, I thought...'

Rex hurried to the door, pulled at the locks and bolts to make sure they were secure. Then he pulled back the same curtain Corinne had been holding only seconds before, and peered out into the darkness.

There was nothing.

Was his mind – or the whiskey – playing tricks on him?

'I'm scared,' said Corinne from behind him.

He held his gaze on the stoop outside for a few seconds more before letting the curtain fall back into place.

'Just sit down and stay away from the window.'

'What do you think it was?'

'Nothing,' he said. 'There's animals out there. We're in the middle of the god damned wilderness.'

He kept the shotgun hanging from his grip like a second limb as he walked back to the kitchen.

He looked out the window again, scanning for movement, and caught another glimpse of his grave and pallid face. Like a ghost staring back at him.

Ghosts were everywhere in the new world. The ghosts of the dead: those killed in the battles and skirmishes all those years ago - wars where people were killed over loaves of bread, bottles of milk and rolls of toilet paper. And the ghosts of those who'd lost their humanity: those who'd been forced to huddle and fend for themselves in diseased pockets of the collapsing country – in ghettoes that echoed with gunfire, in one-horse-towns whose horses had long since deserted them, and in the burnt-out husks of the hyper-infected cities – watching their bodies, and their children's bodies, and their unborn children's bodies mutate before their very eyes.

Turning them into... those things. Those cursed, feral things. The sick and the poor and the hungry and the weak, they'd gone backwards, not forwards. Their genes had collapsed right along with the world. They'd been forced to retreat deep into their DNA and undergo a finger-click-fast transformation that hitherto only insects and deep-sea life had shown themselves capable of performing. A new age of regression; a new species filled not with hunger, but with hate; not with clarity, but with howling confusion.

And here was Rex.

Standing in his kitchen, making tea in his cosy little cabin... jumping at shadows.

He was rattled, but his old friend whiskey was keeping his adrenalin occupied. What a fool he felt. Maybe he'd spent too much time alone. Maybe he'd been drinking too much...

He poured some boiling water into a cup, and left the tea-bag stewing as he entered the adjoining pantry.

It was odd to be staring at empty shelves. He wasn't much of a gardener: he'd never needed to be. He'd always relied on the supplies his people brought to him every couple of weeks (usually along with one or more of his sons). He cursed himself for once in his blasted life not having a contingency plan. If he didn't get a supply re-up soon, he'd be out licking moss from the rocks and trapping rabbits.

Rex surveyed his sparse offerings. There was one biscuit left. One. The batch had been hand-made by one of the chefs in the main camp. Best damn biscuits he'd ever tasted.

He put it on a plate for Corinne.

~~~

He came back into the living room with the tea and biscuit on a small tray, the shotgun gripped and dangling in his other hand.

'I'm sorry about before, I... Thank you for your hospitality.'

'It's okay,' he said, gruffly.

'Who are those three handsome men in the photo up on the stand there? The ones standing with you?' she asked.

'Those are my three boys,' he said, placing the tea and biscuits down on her side table. 'They're stationed down in the valley.'

He sat down, wedging the shotgun between his legs and his chair. His sons hadn't been pleased about his retirement wish, to come up here in self-exile. But he thought they'd understood, or tried their best too, at least. Karl had wanted to come up here with him, but Rex had said no. It was *their* time now, not his. If changing the world had been his remit, then re-building it was theirs. His son's mothers hadn't understood his relocation to the mountain either, but neither had they cared. Rex was fine with that.

'Surprised you didn't see them,' Rex continued. 'Them or my...their people on your way up here. They've got camps and outposts everywhere.'

She shook her head. 'I didn't see anyone. I wish I had.'

'I'll need to have a word with them about that next I see them.'

Corinne looked over at the photograph on the bookcase and smiled a moment. 'Why did they leave you alone up here?'

'My choice.'

'What if you get sick?'

'Then I get sick.'

Corinne leaned back in her chair. 'Can I be honest with you?'

She was a young woman, small in stature, frail, like a new spring flower, but even so, those words – issued from beneath those piercing, shark-like eyes – caused a fist of unease to twist in his gut. He was drawn to whatever confession was coming next, but he dreaded it, too.

'I'm a writer,' she said, dipping her brow bashfully.

Rex laughed, a big, booming laugh that Corinne appeared to interpret as mockery, but was actually relief. Pure, unadorned relief. 'Well,' he said, slapping the sides of his chair. 'The cobwebs are cleared. That actually makes a hell a lot of damned sense, l'il lady. I didn't think we still had those.'

She looked wounded. Brooding.

Rex wiped a smudge of a tear away from one of his eyes. 'If you've got your head in the clouds, you might as well be in the mountains, am I right? Oh, I'm sorry, young 'un, I don't mean to tease, it's just... I shoulda known. What you writing, a love story? I can see it now, two beating hearts cut in two by the mountains, she's in one camp, he's in the other, but, man, their love is too strong to be contained, so she goes to him, over brook and river, hill and valley, because love... well, love's what makes the world go round, ain't it?'

She stared at him, unmoved by his chiding. 'What do *you* think makes the world go round?'

'Men,' he said with a nod, holding his palms up. 'No offence.'

'If you must know I'm writing a history of the world: the world as it was, and the world as it is now. And the world as it will be.'

Rex scoffed. 'If you're writing about the world as it will be, well that ain't history now, is it? 'Less you're psychic too.'

'It's going to be about... everything. Following back the path, seeing where it all went wrong, and following it forwards to the new world. The next world. The better world to come.'

'Now you sound like some religious nut. I been up here in this mountain quite a long time, honey, and I gotta tell you I aint seen God yet.'

Corinne shrugged. 'Maybe he's seen you.'

Rex shook his head. 'I hope you don't mind the question, young 'un, but what would you know about history? The world's, or even your own? You're barely even alive.'

'How about you start by telling me what you did, you know, during the war.'

'How old do you think I am?' he smiled. 'I've never been to war.'

'Millions of people died, my dad said. They starved, they died from the virus, they were... burned, shot... blown up. People were turned into something else and there was fighting, killing. Exterminations. What would you call that if not war?'

'Survival,' said Rex, wishing he had another glass of whiskey. He drained one in his mind. 'You taking notes?'

'I've got a good memory,' she said with a cold smile. 'Hope you don't mind me asking, but... well, are you ashamed of what it cost... for... for people like you to survive?'

Rex felt a whirlpool of irritation whipping in his gut. Here we go again, with that holier-than-thou shit.

'Is that why you've exiled yourself up here on this mountain? Because you're ashamed of what you did? That you couldn't be around your people, or even your sons, anymore because they were a... I don't know, a constant reminder of all that you did and

couldn't take back? That what you're really doing up here is...
hiding.'

Rex could feel his hands starting to tremble.

'Is that what you're doing?' she continued. 'Hiding up here from the
consequences of your actions?'

He stood up, with a speed and a ferocity that surprised him, or it
would have, if he'd had time to think about it. 'God damned
psychiatrist now, too! Lady, all I've heard from your mouth all night
is bullshit, bullshit, bullshit. And whining. And then some more
bullshit. This your idea of gratitude?'

'If you aren't ashamed of what you did, then why are you getting so
angry? Is it because, deep down, you're sorry?'

Rex really was angry. More volcanically angry – and more alive –
than he'd felt in years. He stabbed the air with his finger, felt his
other fist clench into steel. 'Sorry I let you in this god damned
house. What would YOU know about what I did? What any of us
did? The world you've got now – the god damned life you've got,
your daddy's car down there at the bottom of the mountain – you
wouldn't have any of it if it wasn't for people like me.'

Corinne stood up too, her eyes smouldering. 'And what about the
people who didn't make it? What about the people that people like
you killed?'

'They were weak!' bellowed Rex. 'They didn't deserve to make it.
Put that in your god damned history book!'

She was smiling now, but utterly without warmth. 'It didn't take
much for the old man to show his true colours. You've just been

sleeping up here, haven't you? The same snake in a different skin, just like the rest of them.'

Anger pumped at Rex's limbs; before he could process what was happening inside his body he'd yanked up the shotgun like a root. He stood, holding it up at her; could feel his lips curdling into a snarl. Corinne stood firm, all trace of meekness gone.

'That's your answer for everything, isn't it? You just obey your base instincts, like an animal; like a wild *fucking* animal.'

The shotgun shook in his grip, but with fury, not infirmity. He trained its barrel on her head. Pointed it at her eyes.

'Eat your god damned biscuit,' he growled.

She laughed, hysterically and convulsively, bending over double in the process. Rex found himself frozen to the spot, his thoughts clamouring for purchase like a puma trying to mount a landslide. Corinne snatched the biscuit from the plate and held it tightly in her grip.

'You still think I'm one of the changed, don't you? It's the only thing that makes sense to you. No human would deign to criticise the great old general, King of the Mountaintops, Rex the Mighty. And even then, HOW DARE THEY? After all you've done. After all the *sacrifices* you've made.'

How did she know his name? He hadn't told her. He pressed his finger a little harder over the trigger.

'Eat the biscuit, or you'll be eating buckshot,' he said, his words bouncing in his throat like wagons down a trail.

She laughed again. 'The whole world's a western to you, isn't it, Rex? You really want me to eat this biscuit, don't you? Well whaddya gonna do if I don't, huh, sheriff?'

'One,' he said.

The last time she'd hesitated over his instructions he hadn't wanted to pull the trigger. Now, a warm, dark part of him wanted her to defy him; wanted to hear that hee-haw cackle of hers one more time so he could silence it with a quick squeeze of the trigger. Her smile held firm, despite his obvious intent.

'Two.'

He no longer cared who or what she was. Something in him was on its hind legs and roaring. His blood was calling out for blood, a thunder of gunfire to feed his thumping heart. His lips crackled together. His mossy tongue began to push itself against his teeth, but before it could pass through their yellowed gates... she ate it. Pushed that biscuit into her mouth like a parcel along a conveyer belt. Crunched it mechanically with the sharp little pistons of her teeth.

'Three,' she shouted at him, through globs of crumbs. Then she laughed.

Thud! It took Rex a few micro-seconds to process the noise. The sound was cushioned and dream-like, muffled beneath hurling waves of his anger. It was the door. Someone – or something – had struck it.

For a second Rex was frozen to the spot. In his mind's eye, he'd already pulled the trigger, was already looking down on Corinne's collapsed body; a discarded puppet gushing blood from a stump where a head should have been. His skull felt hot, bathed in blaring paraffin. None of it felt real. Not the knock, not Corinne, not the night, the mountain, or the long, stretching river of his past. The door banged again, louder and more insistently this time. He backed away from Corinne - the barrel still aiming at her head - towards the door.

As he fumbled to unfasten the bolts, a little of his senses returned to him. His heart jack-hammered behind his ribcage. One bolt, two bolts, three. He threw open the door, and was greeted by...

Nothing. Only the gathering wind and the pale-fringed darkness beyond. With the barrel of his gun swivelling like a periscope in his hands, he took a few steps outside, with legs that no longer felt like his own. He was floating, rushing, flying out of his body, and out of time itself. Only the machine-gun-rat-a-tat of his heart convinced him of his corporeality.

More ghosts. But ghosts couldn't knock. And there were no trees around, no errant branches to explain the noise. A bird? Something larger? The night was empty, if not entirely still; the wind swayed the tree branches and shook the leaves like glitter. He stood a moment longer, watching for shadows; listening to the whistles and growls of the wind as it whipped its way across the mountain.

He slammed the door behind him again, dead-bolting it quickly. Spun the gun around to Corinne. She was in the seat again, sobbing.

'I'm so scared,' she said, holding her head in her hands.

'Not this shit again,' said Rex, breathing heavily, relaxing his hold on the gun, but not its aim.

'I didn't leave the compound,' she barked at him through her tears, 'I was ordered to leave! By my own father. Told me I was crazy and he couldn't cope with it anymore. Told me if I didn't like life the way it was I should go and see what it was like out there. Told me in the olden days they would've had medicine for someone like me, but since they didn't it was better for everyone if I just left. Said if I didn't leave by myself he'd make me leave!'

She thumped her chest with a clenched fist. 'My own father!'

Her madness was certainly plausible. It would go a long way towards explaining why Rex had never felt entirely comfortable in Corinne's presence; why something about her had never added up.

'How did you know my name?'

Corinne sniffed. 'I think that you underestimate just how famous you are around here. For miles around. My dad said you were a legend. But now they call you, what was it they said… 'The Hermit up on the Hill'.'

Rex processed that for a moment. A hermit? Is that all they said about him? After all he'd done? He cocked his head at Corinne. 'What else did they used to say about me?'

The door knocked again. Then the window; then the other window. Rex spun around, his gun a limp stick in his hand.

'I've brought them here, haven't I?' wailed Corinne. 'Those things, it's them isn't it, they've followed me? I've led them to you! I'm sorry, I'm sorry, I'm sorry…' she wailed, beginning to rock in the chair.

Rex stood slack-jawed, one moment looking at the wall, then the door, then the windows, then the door again, as knock after knock fell upon on the cabin. It wasn't fear he was experiencing, not quite: it was discombobulation; it was the whiskey; it was a refusal to accept that this could be happening. He was safe. He'd made sure he was safe. Protected. This wasn't the way it was supposed to be. Not here.

Not now.

'I'm sorry!' Corinne shrieked, over and over. 'Please, please help me, please don't let them get me! Please help me!'

Each sharp note of her voice stabbed into his brain like a pitchfork. 'SHUT UP!' he roared, clawing at his temples with a trembling hand. 'SHUT UP AND BE QUIET!'

The sound of his own voice, hard and resolute - the voice of the commander he once was, and in truth had never stopped being – shook him from his twisted reverie. If it was the creatures who were massing out there, then he wouldn't run. Or hide. Or even flinch. Skipping between the dread was an excitement - a hunger, almost - to see them; to feel again that promise of power and death singing in his hands.

Corinne sobbed, on and on, as the thuds built to a tattoo on the outside walls and windows, a drumming din that eventually surrounded them on all sides. It might've been a rival faction - maybe Corinne had tricked him, and led a posse of men to his door, ready to kill or ransom the king to gain leverage over his sons in the valley below - but, no. Rex knew that wasn't the case. She wouldn't dare. Nobody in their right minds would dare.

If it was armed men surrounding him now, they would've shouted, made their demands, peppered his shack with bullets, even. These were the creatures – Rex had no doubt about it - their uncomplicated savagery obvious from the animal dirge that was beating on the walls, beating in his ears, thumping in his chest.

'WHO WILL HELP US?' shouted Corinne, 'WHAT ARE WE GOING TO DO?!'

'STAY QUIET!' he roared.

Now, thought Rex, his fingers turning to steel cables, his chest purring like an engine... *Let's have a god damned peek at you, you fucking ugly sons of bitches.*

His chest rose as he threw open the curtains on the first window. There they were. Cloying, roaring, spitting; their numbers legion. Outside, illuminated by the soft light of his lamps, was a solid, sprawling slab of flesh, an almost indistinguishable bluish-grey mass of limbs and teeth and faces, surging and flailing and rocking against each other and the building. The three nearest to the window, their palms and noses pressed against the pane, their mouths opening and closing like razor-toothed fish, lit up with fury when they saw him. Growls and snarls misted the glass.

Rex wasn't worried. It was reinforced glass, the strongest there was. *Good luck smashing through that, you god damned heathens.* To boot, his cabin was built from the hardiest of composite materials, impossible to breach without the use of mechanical or pyrotechnic force. Not to mention that all of his windows, all around the cabin, were closed tight. Too cold out there this time of year. Too many ugly-ass bugs. So, no, he didn't fear the creatures' immediate presence. He felt no more fear than he did when he was a kid at the zoo, tapping on the glass and taunting the tigers.

Maybe the creatures could get inside given enough time; maybe they could simply starve him out. After all, they didn't need to eat. But Rex had something they did not, and would never, have: brains. Damn automatons. He'd have them screaming for their lives sooner rather than later, even if he had to climb up through a hole in the roof and pop them off one at a god damned time.

'I DON'T WANT THEM TO GET IN!' shouted Corinne.

Rex ignored her, and placed his hands and face up to his side of the pane, a smile cracking over his worn lips. As the growls rose in volume and ferocity, in concert with the renewed violence of the palms beating at the glass from the other side, Rex smiled all the harder. What had he ever been so worried about? It was like a wasp sting or a punch in the face; sometimes the idea of it was worse than the reality. He was annoyed at himself for having let such inconsequential ideas get under his skin. Augurs be damned.

'Just like old times, eh, boys?' he said, locking eyes with one of them, staring into its mottled grey sclerae. Rex watched its pupils charge and retreat, charge and retreat, like trapped black animals bashing their heads against their cages.

The drumming and thudding was all around him now, a thunderous storm of anger. Corinne's sobs and wails provided the harmony. Weak girl. He wondered what strength he'd ever seen in her. Just another case of his old mind playing tricks on him; buckling under the boredom and lethargy the years had piled upon his psyche.

No more.

Now he was alive again.

'Corinne!' he shouted, his gaze still locked on one of the creatures. In the sea of limbs and shoulders behind those first creatures, many untold more scrambled for the front, pushing and fighting each other, jostling like insects – a Mexican wave of spastic fury. Rex turned to face Corinne, found her cowering on the armchair, legs drawn in, prostrate with terror.

'Can you move?' he asked her.

She looked up at him, eyes wide and pleading.

'Corinne, can you move?'

She nodded meekly.

'I need you to fetch something for me, can you do that?'

'I...' she started to say, 'I can't go out there.'

Rex laughed. 'No, young 'un, from my room. Down the hall there, past the bathroom. Think you can go for me? I gotta keep an eye on these fellas.' He rapped the glass again, and smiled as the growls and roars rose towards a crescendo.

'What... what do you need?'

'Ammo. More guns. These sons of bitches aren't getting in, but we're gonna need firepower to send them on their way. Lots of it. There's a trunk in my room, down the bottom of the hall, foot of the bed. Bring back what you can. And keep bringing it. I'll tell you when to stop.'

'Th... thank you,' she stuttered, as she clambered to her feet.

'What for?'

'F-for p-protecting me.'

He smiled. 'You're a weird kid, young 'un, but I guess you're *my* weird kid now. When you get home, you tell your daddy 'The Hermit on the Hill' still knows a few tricks. Give 'im my fuckin' business card.'

Corinne nodded and started shuffling towards the adjoining hallway.

'Wait!' said Rex, beckoning her back. 'I want you to come over here first. With me.'

She shook her head, so fast he thought it might dislodge and bounce down onto the wooden floor.

'Come on now, there's nothing to be afraid of. I just want you to see something.'

She came over to him slowly, like a kid on her way to the dentist's chair. As she reached him, he clasped her shoulder and led her gently but firmly to the window, where the creatures were wailing and gnashing. He felt the muscles tighten in her shoulder, felt resistance from her legs and feet.

'Come on, now.'

He held her firmly a foot or so from the window. He couldn't see her face any more, but he could feel her shaking. The creatures suddenly went quiet. Maybe because it was a woman. Maybe because they were spoiling for a fight, and this little urchin didn't look like she had it in her.

'Can you see now?' Rex asked her. 'Look at 'em. They ain't no cause worth fighting for. They ain't no reason to rag on men like me and your daddy. Save the blood in your heart for something real, young un. If you went out there now, they wouldn't pick you up on their god damned shoulders and hail you as their lord and saviour. They'd tear your throat out.'

Corinne didn't say anything, but Rex could feel her breathing; hard and fast and shallow. He gripped her tightly by the shoulder.

'Do you see now?'

'I....' she quivered. 'I sss-seeee.'

He pirouetted her to face him, and placed his hands on her shoulders in a manner he supposed was grandfatherly, or as close to it as he could get. 'It ain't your fault. You didn't live in the old world. You didn't see it die, you didn't have to fight for your life, you didn't have to wonder where your next meal was coming from. You didn't have to keep your children safe from those things out there. But I'm glad you see now.'

He stared into her eyes. They seemed to bulge with clarity. She nodded again, dropped her gaze to the floor. He smiled reassuringly at her as he released the pressure on her shoulders. 'Now go get us some god damned guns.'

He watched as she half-stumbled her way towards the hallway on jellied legs.

Shock can enjoin. Death can entwine.

Bullets can bond.

'She sees,' he whispered to himself.

~~

Corinne staggered down the hallway. She was sweating. Squirming. A solid heat wriggled and churned in her gullet. Rex's bedroom was straight in-front of her, but she hooked a hurried left into the bathroom, just reaching the porcelain as the mush and shards of the biscuit left her mouth in a fountain of slow-drying cement. The taste was noxious. Bitter. The pain was excruciating. She wretched some more, cramming her fingers into her mouth to pull out whatever else was still in there.

She stayed a while hunched over the bowl, breathing hard and fast to distract herself from the searing snake rearing up from the base of her chest all the way up to the top of her throat. She could smell burning. The taste of decay was on her lips. It was on her mind, too. Hatred, hot and furious, burned throughout her body, coursing up her shoulders, tearing at her jaws, crackling between her teeth. She felt fury for the sick world that had died – the world that had passed many years before she'd been born - and for the bastard world that had risen to take its place. She winced. Clenched her jaw. Shook her head. There wasn't any time to waste. The pain would pass.

This moment couldn't.

She tried to stand, but the room was spinning.

As she reeled, thoughts and questions encircled her mind like vultures. She did her best to shoo them away, but her mind was pulsing. Had she shown her hand too early? Did Rex suspect the truth? She knew she should've controlled herself better, but the force of her anger had surprised her with its potency, and it had been difficult to conceal. She hoped her improvisational skills, coupled with Rex's arrogance, had earned her enough time to ensure that none of her people got hurt in what was to come.

What would come next? Not in the next few minutes, but after? What would the new world look like – the 'new' new world, that is? Would it be peaceful? Would she, or her people, ever be able to 'eat'? What did her insides look like? Did she have a stomach, or was it all just wiring: a series of fleshy tubes twisted around aimlessly inside of her, connected only to her heart and the life-giving conductors of her lungs? She had no way of knowing. Her insides – the exact internal structure of all of her kind – was alien to her. Much was. In time they'd learn. They'd learn everything again from scratch, and teach themselves, and the world, some new things into the bargain.

They'd come so far in such a short time. First, the invisible hands of the virus had swaddled her antecedents in cocoons and hatched them out as creatures that were angry, frightened and confused, but better able to survive in the ugly, treacherous jungle the world had become. Another snap had given Corinne, and thousands of new-borns like her, the gift of intelligence, even beauty. Her people weren't animals, or Neanderthals, or savages: they were the ongoing miracle of creation; a picture painted by a perfectionist who was constantly learning new touches, colours and flourishes. Each new coupling was a work of art; every womb a magician's hat of genetic surprises.

Her own family had been killed when she was a child. She had lacked language then, but she'd understood the screams. She'd understood the twisted, terrified look in her mother's eyes as she'd fallen to the ground, her head resting on a carpet of crumbling brown leaves that was quickly stained red. She'd understood the laughter and jeers of the pink-faced men with their sharpened blades and sticks that made sounds like thunder. She'd understood the panic, the desperation, the loss and horror, and she'd certainly understood well enough to run and hide until the savages had left.

She'd spent an unknowable amount of time wandering the hills and forests, scared and alone, until eventually she was taken in by a group of humans who'd found her shivering inside a bush. Because of her pinkish skin and smooth features, they'd mistaken her for one of their own. Perhaps they'd thought her a refugee from a vicious and unprovoked attack by the creatures. In a way, that's exactly what she was.

They'd been kind to her at first, but their devotion had only lasted as long as it had taken for them to work out that she wasn't human. Or, at least, not as human as *they* were. She ceased to be a vulnerable little girl, and became instead a goblin that would one day grow strong enough to tear their throats out while they slept. People gathered in the streets to shout and scream at her. A few had thrown stones and rocks.

One of the men had bundled Corinne into his jeep. He'd driven her far beyond the fringes of his camp's boundaries, and pushed her out on a road that stretched for endless, hazy miles in either direction. She hadn't understood at first, but then he'd fired his thunder stick into the air, a booming, hollow roar that had put her on her heels, and sent her fleeing in a blur of panic.

Though she'd lacked the words to construct the truth of her feelings, afterwards she'd felt sad, angry, betrayed. It didn't occur to her until years later that this man had probably saved her from the baying mob in the camp.

She'd wandered again after that. Weeks. Months. Years. She had no way of knowing. Sometimes she encountered humans, sometimes her own kind; sometimes they were in groups, sometimes they were alone. Almost without exception she was treated as an outcast, vermin, and chased away with either teeth or guns.

Over the years that followed she learned how to get close to people without being seen; how to study them in silence. One fateful day - she guessed she must have been around eleven or twelve - she'd been crouching in a tree in a newly discovered patch of woodland when a member of her own kind, a boy of similar age, had padded softly into the thicket.

She watched him gathering up sticks and investigating some insects and small rodents that were bustling through the undergrowth and crawling up the tree-bark. His skin was a light hue of blue, identifying him more closely with the true-breed she so clearly wasn't. As she watched him – fondly, curiously – the truth of his intelligence shone from him, in the gentleness and simple thoughtfulness he brought to bear on his surroundings.

He came to the wood at the same time each day. She always made sure she was there, too. She loved watching him; fascinated by his fascination. One day, shifting her posture to shake life back into a deadening leg, she'd misjudged her footing on a branch, and sent it snapping to the ground. She grabbed for a higher branch, steadied herself, then recoiled in panic, and shimmied round to the far side of her tree to hide.

The wood fell silent for a few moments. She was ready to spring and flee, but the boy called out to her; not in a way that presaged anger or threats, but softly, and in human English. Corinne had picked up a few words and phrases over the years, but she could tell that the boy was as fluent as he was confident. She shimmied slowly around the trunk again to where she'd been standing, so she could look down at him again. He was smiling up at her. Before she had time to think, she was already smiling back.

'Come down,' he said. 'Please. I won't hurt you.'

His voice was soft. Warm. After a few frozen moments she clambered down from the tree and stood – bunched and awkward – just a few feet away from him. His name was Leaf, he told her, a name he'd given himself.

'I... not... name,' she stuttered.

'You can be Corinne,' he told her. 'I heard it said once. I think when some humans were reading from a book. I remembered it. It's nice, don't you think?'

She agreed the name sounded nice. She would have agreed to any name he'd offered.

'What...' she said, struggling to spit the words out. 'What... is book?'

Over the years that followed Leaf and Corinne met together in the wood every day. Leaf taught her the basics of human language, and shared with her all he knew of, and was still learning about, mankind, not to mention the tentative history of their own fragile people. Every now and then he would try to invite her back to his group as his guest, keenly and insistently, but she always resisted. A lifetime of rejection tends to cultivate a sensitivity to it, especially when that rejection has been married with violence. Besides, what she was experiencing with Leaf for the very first time - that bond, that simple fact of acceptance, was too intoxicating to share for fear of diluting it, or, worse, losing it altogether. She wanted to be with Leaf. No-one else. She was happy around him. For the first time she was happy.

Sometimes they'd go to a nearby lake and watch the sun as it shimmered over the water, its perfect brilliance only occasionally disturbed by leaping fish, who'd dazzle themselves in the rays of the sun before slapping back down with a precision plop; silvery circus performers putting on a show just for them.

Corinne often followed Leaf back to his group, always unobserved. She'd climb a tall tree and watch him at play with his friends and family, observe their strange and wonderful rituals and behaviours.

The group seemed wary and skittish sometimes, which was understandable given the humans and their destructive ways, but they were happy. Sometimes they sang; songs that seemed to last for hours; wordless refrains that had more in common with birdsong than anything the human throat seemed capable of producing. Their songs rose up to reach her, sonorous and beautiful, enveloping her in such clouds of bliss that she'd often forget the long road of loneliness that had led her from there to here.

She knew something was wrong when he didn't turn up at the wood that day. Their companionship had a rhythm, unspoken but never broken - not in all the years they'd bonded - and its absence carried the weight and sadness of an upended oak tree.

She ran from the wood, up the slope of the hill, through another wood, her thoughts racing, her heart pounding, all the while birds exploding into the sky in great pockets, charting the urgent, winding path of her agony. It was a journey she never wanted to complete; even in her primal terror she'd been cogent enough to wish to stay forever in that eternal present, never to see what lay at the edge of that thundering panic.

As long as she was running, he'd be alive. As soon as she stopped...

Where songs had once danced in the air around Leaf's camp – it wasn't a camp; it was a home – there was only silence, bathed in smoke. Charred and bloodied limbs were scattered on the ground like road-kill; bodies lay twisted and wrecked, their eyes searching the mud and the heavens both for help that never came. She trod softly, as if her careless footfalls could still hurt them. She stepped over an old woman, her tattered clothes burned and spattered, the brilliant blue of her neck scarred a deep crimson; she passed a child

– a child of no more than eight, her skin the same pinkish hue as hers – hugging her knees in a sad and pitiful frieze of her final moments. The ground was blackened and burnt; some of the trees had been peppered with bullets, others still had been half-wrenched from the ground as though by an angry giant.

She searched for Leaf, each body she scanned that wasn't his filling her first with relief, then revulsion, then gnawing, nauseating guilt that she'd wished them dead a second time. She found a feeling swirling in her thoughts that she had no idea had an equal in human language: widow. She felt it, but didn't know how to speak it. She was a widow now. Only at this moment had she realised how deeply she'd felt for Leaf, how inextricably bound she'd been to him. And now the moment was gone.

He was gone.

Leaf was gone…

She found him at the base of a tree. There wasn't even a body she could hug and hold. Just a head, its mouth gaping, frozen open in horror. Lips that had once sang and laughed and shouted with joy now hung empty, their ridges marked with blood and incipient rot. It wasn't Leaf anymore. There was nothing left she could say goodbye to. Just a thing. A fragment. A dead piece of him.

Leaf's eyes stared up into the canopy behind her. A wail escaped Corinne's lips, a piercing, rolling howl of agony that sliced through the sepulchral silence, and left the air ringing with sadness. She couldn't leave him. She couldn't let anyone see him like this.

She scrambled in the dirt at the base of the tree like a frenzied dog, wrenching up soil and leaves, grabbing up great clumps at a time, her fingers black with mulch and dirt. She couldn't bear to have those lifeless pearls gaping up at her: she wanted to bury him, her feelings, this moment, the world itself - bury it until it choked on its own stink.

She slept there that night at the base of the tree, next to the mound under which lay the last earthly traces of Leaf. As darkness fell she sang a song she'd once heard Leaf's mother sing. It echoed out over the cold wilderness beyond the trees, and was soon heard by a wandering band of others like her. They went to her, followed the trail of her sad lament, and stayed with her there in the darkness, joining her in song. This was a scene they'd been a part of more times than they knew how to count. A scene they resolved, there and then, never again to bear witness to.

In the long, cold years that followed, Corinne built upon the foundations that Leaf had laid for her. She became cleverer still, stronger, faster, more cunning. She travelled the towns and mountains seeking out others like her and allying them to her cause, uniting the smart and the slow, the pink and the blue, alike under one banner. Building an army. Pulling together the first parts of the body of a new civilisation, starting with the fists.

She slipped away to surveil the enemy, taught others to do the same. In time she could pass herself off as fully human; knew what to do, and what not to do, to avoid their scrutiny.

How to infiltrate them.

How to trick them.

How to destroy them.

...How she despised them. Over many years and across hundreds, perhaps even thousands, of mountain miles, Rex's name and crimes had come up time and again. The Mountain King; the Hermit on the Hill; the bogeyman.

Now she'd found him, and he was nothing more than a frightened and pathetic old man, probably months from death. A drunk. A recluse. A broken shadow of the great solid rock his legend had pronounced him as. She'd make him taste his own obsolescence before the night was done; force him to feel the dying screams of his entire twisted race as she wiped their scourge from the face of the freshly emptied earth.

Rex hadn't killed her family, or Leaf – her beloved, long-gone Leaf...

But he might as well have.

They *all* might as well have.

She stood up, unfastened her trousers and wrenched the rubber prosthesis from her crotch, tossed it to the floor. She looked down on it with disgust. The old world had produced this. A fake slit and asshole, not for any medical benefit, but for pleasure: to give sad, lonely humans something to abuse and desecrate on cold, lonely nights. Who were the true animals here? The real freaks?

Corinne looked down and saw a roll of toilet-paper skewered and stuck to the wall by a metal frame. She swiped at it with her hand and watched as it spun around and around, the sheets unravelling like paper innards spilling to the floor.

She reached up to the bathroom window, and clicked the lock. She pushed it open, and as she did so a sonorous wave of growls and hisses sped through the opening, quickly flooding and enveloping the tiny room.

~~

The creatures were almost biting through the glass in their frenzy to reach Rex's grinning face. He slammed on the window with his fist to agitate them further. He lifted the barrel of his shotgun and slotted it against the pane, square with one of their skulls.

'It really is good to see you,' he laughed. A smile dashed across his face, as close in hue to fondness as Rex was capable of conveying. 'This,' he said, tapping the glass with his knuckles, 'calls for a toast.'

Gun in hand, he strode to the back of the room, snatched up a fresh glass and poured himself another whiskey, rested the shotgun against the cabinet. There was an attic of sorts above him, a glorified crawl space really, with a small window that in more agile years he'd climbed through to get on the roof and clean out the gutters, or even just to drink and sunbathe when the opportunity presented itself. The plan was formed. He'd get Corinne to keep an eye on the critters down here and keep their attention focused on the windows, as he pulled himself up there and started picking them off from the roof. He'd even take a bottle of the good stuff up there with him, for old time's sake.

The whiskey tasted purer, sweeter somehow as it funnelled down his throat; more like a liqueur than the gut-rot it actually was. Rex was changing, minute to minute. He could feel it. He was growing in strength. The evening had brought about a re-invigoration of body and spirit, a re-birth almost. It wasn't the booze. Correction, it wasn't *only* the booze. He'd had booze all his days – so much and so often that it was almost a baseline. No, he felt strong and renewed because he had *purpose* again. *Finally* he had purpose again. Adrenaline once more surged through the rusted engine of his body, and now he had somewhere to channel the power it stirred. And he planned on putting it right into the heads of those godless fucking beasts out there. He'd take his shotgun, a rifle or two, perhaps even an old grenade – yeah, he was pretty sure he still had a few of those littered around – and he'd exterminate them, one by one, batch by batch, and watch as dominoes of blood blasted through them like spray-paint. Fountains here, geysers there, great gushing rivers of blood, erupting like volcanoes. He'd leave an autumnal carpet of reds and pinks to greet the dawn sun when next it rose above the dark, hunched shoulders of the mountains.

He was a commander again, too, albeit a commander with only one soldier at his disposal. Corinne. The little girl he'd mistaken for a wolf. But she was a lamb. Firm-footed but soft-throated, ready to be brought to heel and bonded with him through blood. His groin stirred. Oh, but she was such a pretty little thing, so taut and tentative, her wide and innocent eyes empty of all but the dark reflection of his own eyes. Maybe come dawn she'd be thankful for her life. Ready to join an old general in his bed to greet the new day with some fire in her belly. His fire: the promise of his seed flowing into her like the recipe to life itself. Send her back to her daddy with the Mountain King's baby inside of her, a new prince and heir to consolidate his power over the realm. Retirement could wait.

It was time to reclaim his throne.

'Corinne!' he beamed, as he caught her from the corner of his eye walking in from the hallway. It took him a second to register the rifle that was in her grip. Not nervously coddled, not clumsily dangled, but held, comfortably and securely, its barrel pointing directly at his chest. He instinctively grabbed for the shotgun, his whiskey glass tumbling to the floor like a duelling glove. CRACK-BOOM! He flinched and fell back as shards of wood flew from the cabinet, and the glass splintered at his feet. A few pictures of his sons tumbled from the top of the unit and slammed, face first, to the floor. Another report sent Rex dodging towards the kitchen. But he didn't get far.

'One more step and you're dead.'

He stopped, his back to her, his chest rising and falling as he desperately tried to catch some air in his lungs.

'Turn around,' she said. 'Don't worry, I won't make you take your pants off.'

Rex stood, his thoughts quickly swirling from a storm to the funnelled precision of a tornado. She wanted him to turn around. He wouldn't. The mind was the greatest weapon in combat, and he'd use it to his advantage.

'Will this bit be goin' in the book, young 'un?'

'I won't ask again.'

'What is it that you want?'

'I want you. To turn around.'

Her tone was one of clipped fury. Good. Let her anger knock her off balance. He lifted his hands aloft in a gesture of mock submission.

'See, if you wanted me dead you'd have shot me in the back. So what is it? You drag a herd of these things up here to scare me? I 'aint scared. Not of you, not of them.'

His heart was slowing down, but still pressing against the inside of his chest like a man moving – or desperately trying to move – a heavy boulder up a hill with his back.

'One,' she said.

Rex thought he could detect the word being chiselled through the aperture of a smile.

'Two...'

His heart kept pushing. No faster. No slower. 'So this is a coup, is it? Your daddy waiting out there to scoop me up off the floor?'

'Three.'

'Best place to shoot is right at the base of the fuckin' skull.'

Rex could hear footsteps. Creaks. Low growling...lots of it, building in spread and pitch, forming a semi-circle - a damn-near chorus-line - around Corinne. If those things were in here, too; if they'd somehow found a way, then maybe they'd buy him precious enough seconds to reach his gun before they'd finished tearing her asunder.

'You wanna do it up to ten? I don't feel rested yet.'

Any moment now, he thought, he'd hear the scream, the rips, the tears, the howls for mercy, which he'd blot out with a few blasts of the shotgun, careful not to disturb whichever of the creatures were making putty of her flesh.

'NO!' shouted Corinne, and in that finger-click of a second, Rex spun around, dropped his arms, and reached down and out with his leg and hands towards the gun. Then he stopped. He stopped dead.

The creatures weren't attacking Corinne; instead, they were deferring to her. Her left arm was outstretched and pushing into the chest of a creature standing by her side, holding it back as it growled at Rex, its chest flexing in fury. She released the pressure and returned the free hand to the rifle.

Two creatures flanked her, and behind them a snarling mass of the damn things, a shifting colour-chart of pinks and blues, some of them wearing clothes, some rags, some naked, all of them sprung on their haunches as if awaiting a command. Rex stood up straight, stared at Corinne, not sure what to do or say next. What the hell was happening?

'Unlock the door,' she said, holding Rex's gaze.

'I will not.'

'I wasn't talking to you.'

A hulking, pinkish creature with a ridged forehead, wearing only shorts and a tatty shirt, broke ranks from behind Corinne, and moved towards the door, glancing over at Rex with a baleful glower as he did so.

'Murderer,' mumbled the creature.

Rex flinched.

Then smiled.

'So you've taught these fuckin' dipshits how to talk? We'll add animal trainer to your list of talents.'

The pink creature at the door stopped, its muscles tightening.

'No,' said Corinne, softly.

The creature slid back the bolts and threw open the door, a chill swooping into the room along with six of the creatures, who took up position a few feet from Rex, where they stood baring their teeth.

The open door acted as a loudspeaker for the thunderous din outside, broadcasting the creatures' anger and disgust into every corner of the lounge area, which was now swollen and alive with roars, yells, thumps and chitters. The two creatures he'd taunted at the window-pane stood a little closer than the others, their blue faces twisted with rage, their eyes incandescent with hatred. Big Pink stood at the side of them like a ringmaster.

Why were they not attacking him? Why were they not attacking Corinne? How was she doing this?

Rex felt a jolt behind his knees, an elevator dropping suddenly between floors, but managed to keep himself steady, the merest of micro-stumbles betraying his projection of calm. So much adrenalin now, the whiskey felt like it was almost entirely washed from his system. All that adrenalin and nowhere to put it.

The creatures wouldn't move, he *couldn't* move, but still his body kept pumping out urgent messages to his heart, his fists, his legs. He had to stay focused; had to hold on to whatever strength he still possessed and not show a single quiver of weakness, however much his assessment of the tactical situation had been turned on its head, and however fast his heart – quickly and painfully now - had started beating. If he had any hope of seeing dawn, he had to radiate as much dominance, or at least insouciance, as possible.

'Fellas, glad you could make it to the shindig, but didn't I say black tie? You aint gonna like this, neither, but you just missed the last of the biscuits.'

Corinne turned to one of the creatures who'd been snapping at Rex through the window. 'Take his gun.'

It loped towards Rex, passed within a few feet of him, snatched up the shotgun, then loped back to where it had been standing. It held the gun pointing up at the ceiling, and stood shaking it like a medicine man's rattle.

'Any more weapons?' asked Big Pink.

Corinne kept her eyes - and the rifle – centred on Rex as she answered Big Pink. 'Down the hall behind me, the room straight ahead. Whole chest of them. Take someone with you, get it out of here.'

Big Pink headed towards the hallway behind Corinne. One of the nearby creatures broke formation and followed him.

Rex thudded his chest. 'If you're gonna kill me, just fuckin' kill me!'

Corinne took a step towards him. 'You'd like that, wouldn't you, Rex? The Martyr on the Mountain.'

'All this screwing around, hiding in the bushes, drinking tea, putting on a god damned show with these freaks, just do what you came here to do and leave me to fuckin' rot in peace.'

Corinne smiled. Next she issued an almost wistful chuckle. 'It's not a nice feeling, is it, Rex? Being helpless. I'm glad you're scared though.'

Rex balled his fists, wrapped his knuckles around invisible bars, then used them to pull himself forward a few inches, the force of the adrenalin almost toppling him over as he surged. The creatures moved in unison - from in-front of him, from the side - growling like a pack of tigers putting a hoofed beast in its place. They stamped the ground with their feet as if to mark the boundaries of Rex's invisible prison cell, and he stopped - though his organs kept moving, pumping, churning, beating, thumping.

'I aint scared of dying! I'll greet it with a smile on my lips.'

'Oh, Rex,' said Corinne, in a way that would've been almost pitying if not for the smile. 'There are far worse things in this world than death. Just ask the people who couldn't get food or medicine after the plague struck. Just ask the people who were left to fend for themselves in the sealed cities as their own lungs choked them, or they starved to death. Just ask the people whose bodies changed before their very eyes, and who found themselves and their children hounded and hunted across the wilderness: never able to settle, never able to rest. But you can't ask them, can you? Because most of them are dead. Killed, Rex. By people like you.'

'Oh, boo god-damned hoo. This shit again?' He gestured at the hate-filled creatures surrounding him. 'What are you, a social worker for these things? Look at 'em. Even if they had an ass they wouldn't know how to scratch it. They *do* know how to kill though, right? God damned killing machines, the lot of them. Ugly, vicious sons of bitches.'

'We're not like you!' seethed Corinne stamping a foot on the floor.

Rex felt emboldened now. He didn't want to die, but neither did he want to live, if living was part of Corinne's plan. Better willingly to stroll into the jaws of death than submit to wasting away at your enemy's whim. He left his prison and walked over to the second of the creatures from the window, the one that hadn't gone off to steal his guns. The room rose up with mutters and snarls. He could see they were rattled, fighting against the fences Corinne's commands had built around them. He could see Corinne following him with the rifle, a look of alarm on her face.

'You!' said Rex, coming so close to the creature he could smell its sharp, acrid breath. It peeled back its lips like a baboon, its chiselled teeth yammering in its gums. 'I bet you'd like to reach inside my throat with those grubby l'il fuckin' fingers of yours, wouldn't you? Well, why don't you just do it, boy? Creatures in my day wouldn't have no pink-skinned wummin tellin' em what to do. You lost your balls as well as your asshole?'

'GET AWAY FROM HIM!' shouted Corinne.

'You know,' said Rex, drawing closer still, almost eyeball to eyeball with the creature. He could almost feel its body shaking, the heat from its mouth. 'I'll bet I killed your grandpa, maybe even your daddy. Me and my boys used to travel all over these parts stomping out your fuckin' nests wherever we found them. Saw it as sport. Used to keep tally. "Got another one, dad," my boys would say, "One less godless abomination out here pollutin' the earth." Once I even put a grenade in...'

The creature reached out for him with its hands, but before it could grab him, another set of arms barrelled into Rex, picking him up like a sack of meat and propelling him across the room, slamming him against the unit at the far wall. Big Pink. He'd come back into the room with the chest of guns, dropped it to the floor with a thud and rescued Rex - if rescue was even the right word. Rex lay on the ground, the pain driving punches up his spine from his lower back, crushed fragments of ornaments and pieces of shelving smashed everywhere around him.

Big Pink was standing above him, his shoulders rising and falling like waves, his nostrils flaring. Corinne strode over, and shoved the rifle in Big Pink's hand. She bent down level with Rex, her face once again a mask.

'Oh Rex,' she said. 'You're a cowboy to the end, aren't you?'

Rex winced. Laid his hands flat on the ground to take the weight – and the pain – from his back. 'What did you mean "we're not like you"?' he asked. 'You got so cosy with these things you think you are one now?'

She shook her head. 'All night you suspected me of being non-human, and now that the truth is literally staring you in the face you won't accept it. Is it your pride, Rex? Would your defeat be easier to bear if I was human?'

'You can't be one of 'em. You sound...' he winced again, a jolt going up his spine. '...smarter than some... people I know.'

Her lip curled. 'People change. Sometimes whole peoples change. Yours went down, ours went up. If you hadn't spent your whole life trying to kill us, maybe you'd know a little bit more about us. Maybe this wouldn't be happening to you now.'

'But... you showed me, before you came into my house, you pulled down your...'

'Fake,' she said. 'Just like your hospitality.'

Rex laughed; lay back against the busted unit and laughed some more, hysteria coming out of him in waves. She watched him, almost impassively, as a bird would an insect.

'So what now?' asked Rex, his laughter dying, his fight fading.

'Now?' Corinne reached out and grabbed Rex by the throat. He could feel himself choking as she applied more pressure, but he did nothing to resist her grip. 'Now you get to see the world-to-come I was talking about.'

Rex sat gasping and coughing as Corinne released the pressure on his gullet. She sprang to her feet, pushed past the small crowd of creatures by the door and disappeared outside the cabin. He was left with a room of hate-filled eyes, all locked on and burning into him. He didn't hold their collective gaze for long, looked down at his feet instead. The log fire was out now, though hell apparently didn't need heat to prevail. It was right here in his cabin. And the demons were real.

He realised why his fight had gone. Not just because he was an old man lying crumpled beneath the bulk of his worldly possessions; outsmarted and outnumbered in the sanctity of his own home, or reeling from the almost cast-iron reality that he'd supped his last whiskey - although all of those possible explanations carried weight - but because somewhere in his psyche, a wall was crumbling, its pieces blown away like dust.

He knew why he hadn't mentioned his people, his sons; why he hadn't run at the creatures invoking their names and threatening brutal and bloody revenge. He knew why, but still couldn't bring himself to say it out loud, even within the confines of his own head. But he knew: knew why his people hadn't made their last supply run; understood the low probability of a force of hundreds of the creatures slipping by them undetected to catch him unawares in his cabin. Rex winced again, but not because of his back or hips. He was in the process of rebuilding that wall, brick by fragile brick, when Corinne pushed her way back into the cabin carrying a large black trash bag, heavy and bulging. Rex looked up at her.

She wasn't smiling.

'This is what we leave you with. Your empire is in this bag, Rex. And I hope you feel the pain of that for every single wretched day you have left on this earth.'

She dropped the bag at his feet; arched her lips into a grimace. Looked down at the floor.

'I thought this moment would make me feel happier.'

She turned her back on him and started towards the door. Rex watched her, the black bag wavering at his feet like a mirage. She stopped, heaved her shoulders and bellowed out a command that belied her small stature, but was entirely befitting of the lion he now knew roared within her chest. Her true voice; the one she'd kept hidden from him.

'TAKE EVERYTHING.'

Rex watched her golden hair disappear in a blur of pink and blue muscle, as the creatures spun and lurched past her through the door, tripping and thundering into each other as they spilled into the cabin. They barrelled towards the kitchen, down the hall, swarmed all over the room, picking, shoving and smashing, grabbing and swiping armfuls of ornaments and pictures from the shelves, even from the broken unit at his back. Some of them trampled on his legs, like he was an insect under their feet. He got the sense that his home, his things, his life were a proxy for his body, which doubtless they'd prefer to be tearing apart instead. There was a blur of legs and torsos all around him, a din of scuffles and thumps. Even with the concert of limbs passing to and fro, and the orchestra of tinkles, crashes, growls, bangs and splinters erupting all around him, still the universe kept receding, its soundtrack dimming, until all that was left was him and the bag.

The creatures scurried through the main room and out into the mountain night in a riot of rasping laughter, carrying kitchen appliances and utensils, the last of the food, bottles of whiskey, bed-linens, covers, clothes, rugs, mats, paintings, knives, guns, keepsakes, clutter – everything he owned or had ever held dear. One of them hurled a table at a window and was momentarily confused, and more than a little disappointed, when it thudded from the pane and bounced back onto the floor. He leapt on it instead, cracking it into pieces, before scattering its parts like bones.

Soon the room was empty.

And silent.

And Rex crawled towards the bag, reached out his hands to grasp it and...

'Dad.'

His son's voice.

Little Karl.

The dreamer. The protector. Advocate for the voiceless, wherever he found them, whoever they were: whether they slithered on their bellies through the tall grass, lowed in the meadows, or walked on two legs; whether they were pink, black, brown... or blue.

Rex looked down into his son's bluest of blue eyes and laid a big hand on his bony little shoulder.

Karl looked up at him, almost defiantly, the only person in the camp who could get away with fixing him with that sort of a look. 'What are you going to do with her?'

The little girl had arrived in camp, shivering and afraid, after being found in the forest by a routine patrol. After the doctor had checked her over, they'd left her in a camp-bed in the surgery. A creature attack, was everyone's best guess. The kid was so scared she couldn't talk, and any time she tried to talk it came out as incoherent mush. The doc stayed close, but not so close as to crowd her. Everyone reckoned she just needed some time alone in a place where she knew she was safe, to give her time to start *feeling* that she was safe. Karl – that fearless, big-hearted boy - hadn't considered that the 'rules' might also have applied to him. He wanted the little girl to know that she had a friend, and he defied any of the adults to stop him, his father included.

When Karl slipped into the surgery he found the little girl not on her camp-bed, but huddled in the far corner of the room on the opposite side from the bed. Karl had brought her a gift, a soft teddy bear, given to him by his mother, that he'd hugged to sleep when he was a very young boy.

Rex was watching from the other side of the room's high window, unseen by either of them. He was worried about his son's empathy and where it might lead him, but also impressed by his single-mindedness.

Karl stood for a long time - quietly, patiently - holding the bear at arm's length. When the little girl started to get visibly anxious, he sat down on the floor, crossed his legs, and gently pushed the bear towards her, where it drifted to a stop almost half-way between them. Rex could see Karl holding up his hands, pointing at the bear, and talking softly to the girl. The boy wasn't daunted. He was patient. And kind.

After a long stand-off, the girl crawled towards Karl, moving more like a cat than a child. She padded at the teddy. Sniffed it. Touched it. Rolled it around in her hands. Eventually, she sat cross-legged on the floor, facing Karl, and slid the teddy back to him across the floor. Both children laughed. He slid the bear back again, and the two children sat for an age - Rex watching them all the while; smiling, actually smiling – passing the bear back and forth, back and forth, with simple childish glee. Words would only have been an encumbrance. They didn't need them.

For the first time, the little girl looked unafraid. She looked happy.

A little later, of course, the doctor discovered that the little girl wasn't a little girl at all, but one of them. A creature. Her age brooked no exemption with the people in the camp: a tiger was a tiger; a rat was a rat.

A creature was a creature.

'Dad?' Karl said again, when his father didn't respond. 'Don't let them kill her.'

Life had hardened Rex's heart to all except danger, but Karl had a way of massaging conscience back into his ventricles, even for just the briefest of moments. Sometimes the boy's innocence was as unwelcome as it was infectious, but there were times... so many times... when Rex just wanted his little boy to be right.

About the world.

About him.

Rex leaned down to whisper into Karl's ear: 'I promise. You hear me? I promise. But you can't talk about this with anyone. You hear me? Ever. But I won't let anyone hurt the girl.'

He'd taken the girl himself, swept her up from the jaws of the mob, who'd demanded instant and deadly action, a purge to help them sleep better at night, and taken her out in his jeep, far, far away from the camp, promising he'd do the deed and dump the body so the children wouldn't have to see it, or even think about it.

But instead he'd let her go. Pushed her out on to some hot, dusty road. Fired his gun in the air to set her on her heels, and to warn her: stay away from human beings, or next time you won't be as lucky.

She'd looked back at him only once as she'd staggered down that baked asphalt highway, with a look in her eyes that seemed at once childish and ancient, pleading and promising, hurt and hateful.

He couldn't bear to look into those eyes…

Those god damned eyes…

~~

He looked down into Karl's eyes. No longer the bluest of blue, but open and grey. Rex closed them.

There were two other heads in the bag.

But Karl's was the only one Rex wanted to hold.

~~

Corinne moved through the darkness, eyes attuned to the murk, aware of the fanning army of soldiers – friends, lovers, family – flanking her on both sides, the trudging noise of their feet through the mountain grass speaking of their solidity. Their unity.

They marched as one. Acted as one. She would lead them, but only until they no longer needed her. She was teaching them to lead themselves. The guns they'd destroy. Most of them anyway. They were weapons of the old world, responsible for so much death and hatred. They wouldn't need them.

The new humans – for that's what her and her people were – would have no need to hoard, or consume. They wouldn't have to scar the planet, or slaughter its creatures, to make food. They could just live; they could just simply be.

But only once the old world had been swept away.

She saw in the darkness ahead reflections of the fire that was now flickering from the giant turbine behind Rex's cabin, and as she turned back to look she was greeted by whoops of triumph from a group of her people standing at its base. Flames curled up the turbine's wooden column like ivy, the burning hand of nature come to sear away its rivals.

She stood awhile, gazing into the flames; listened as they crackled and roared, and as her people's axes clanged and thudded into the wood. Moments later the turbine creaked, bent, then toppled, falling as if in slow motion, arcing towards the ground. It rested its fiery head with a crash on the forest floor. Orange tongues reached out to lick the leaves, the fire moving, first in a wave, now a sea that was rising, lapping, flowing inexorably towards the cabin. The rest of her people ran to join her, hooting and cackling with glee, their faces flickering masks of orange.

Corinne turned her back: on the cabin; on the past; on the old world; on Rex's plaintive howls that rose in concert with the thundering roar of the fire, his screams soon rebounding in the darkness, and echoing across the mountain top.

She knew what shape the new world would take. It would be better. It would be fairer.

It would be kinder.

Printed in Great Britain
by Amazon